WITHDRAWN

Jane Clarke & Britta Teckentrup

NEON LEON

nosy crow

Leon is a chameleon.

He's in this picture.

Which chameleon do you think is Leon?

Chameleons can change colour
to **match** wherever they go.

Where do you think the chameleons are off to?
Let's turn the page
and find out.

The chameleons are in a leafy jungle.
And they've all turned **green!** They **match!**
They're hard to spot, aren't they?

Well, all except for Leon.
He's still **orange.**

What do you think will happen when the chameleons go to a **sandy** desert?

Yes! They **match.**
The chameleons have
all turned **yellow!**

Well, all except for Leon.
He's still **orange!**

Hmm . . . let's see if Leon can do any
better in the big, **grey**, rocky mountains.
Can you help him this time? Tell Leon
what colour he should turn.

I don't think he can hear you.
Can you say it **louder**?

All the chameleons are hidden among the rocks.
They **match** . . . but has Leon changed colour?
No, he's still **very orange**. Poor Leon.

Maybe he'll feel better after a good
night's sleep back in the jungle.
Let's say, "Goodnight, Leon," and softly turn the page.

Oh dear. Leon's so **bright** he's keeping all the other chameleons awake! What a **lot** of grumpy chameleons!

And Leon looks
very **sad** . . .

But **where's** Leon going now?
Do you think he's looking for
somewhere he can fit in?

Look! He's found the perfect place already.
Everyone here is **orange,** just like Leon!

He matches!

But, oh no! The birds are flying up, up, up into the bright **blue** sky. Maybe they've gone to find something to eat.

And now Leon doesn't fit in any more.

Whisper, "Don't worry, Leon. Everything will be okay."

But what's that over there in
the corner of the page?
Could it be something . . .

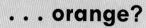 **. . . orange?**

Hurry, Leon!

But Leon can't walk very fast, can he?
We'd better give him a bit of time.
Let's count to **ten**, then turn the page . . .

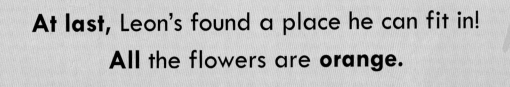

At last, Leon's found a place he can fit in!
All the flowers are **orange.**

And look! Leon's **happy.**

Let's all clap our hands and
smile, smile, smile with him.

But there's one thing that would make Leon
even **happier.** Can you guess what that is?

That's right! Leon's found a **friend.**
Can you spot them both?

It's the perfect match.

To Angelina and
Sammy – J.C.

For Sanja – B.T.

First published in 2017
by Nosy Crow Ltd
The Crow's Nest
10a Lant Street
London SE1 1QR
www.nosycrow.com

ISBN 978 0 85763 806 9

Nosy Crow and associated logos
are trademarks and/or
registered trademarks of
Nosy Crow Ltd

Text © Jane Clarke 2017
Illustrations © Britta Teckentrup 2017

The right of Jane Clarke to be identified
as the author of this work and of Britta Teckentrup
to be identified as the illustrator of this work
has been asserted.

All rights reserved

This book is sold subject to the condition that it shall not, by
way of trade or otherwise, be lent, hired out or otherwise
circulated in any form of binding or cover other than that
in which it is published. No part of this publication may be
reproduced, stored in a retrieval system, or transmitted
in any form or by any means (electronic, mechanical,
photocopying, recording or otherwise) without the prior
written permission of Nosy Crow Ltd.

A CIP catalogue record for this book is available
from the British Library.

Printed in China by Imago

Papers used by Nosy Crow are made from
wood grown in sustainable forests.

1 3 5 7 9 8 6 4 2